Come to My Party

MACMILLAN PUBLISHING COMPANY *New York*
Maxwell Macmillan Canada *Toronto*
Maxwell Macmillan International
New York Oxford Singapore Sydney

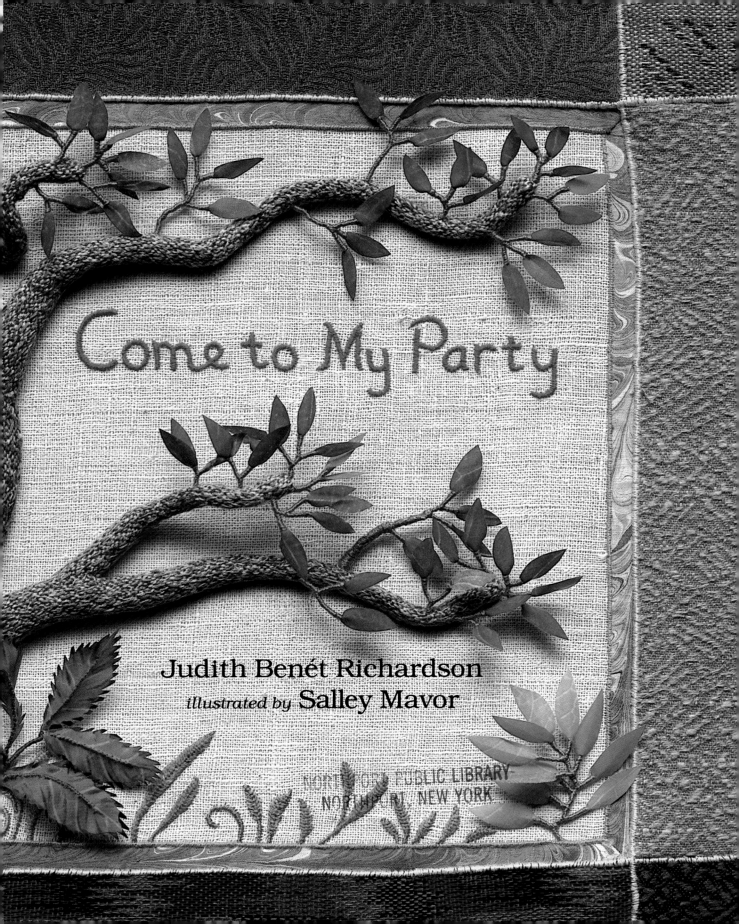

Come to My Party

Judith Benét Richardson
illustrated by Salley Mavor

Macmillan Publishing Company is part of the Maxwell Communication
Group of Companies.

Macmillan Publishing Company, 866 Third Avenue, New York, NY 10022

Maxwell Macmillan Canada, Inc., 1200 Eglinton Avenue East, Suite 200,
Don Mills, Ontario M3C 3N1

First edition
Printed in the United States of America
1 3 5 7 9 10 8 6 4 2
The text of this book is set in 18 pt. ITC Bookman Light.
The illustrations are rendered in fabric relief.

Library of Congress Cataloging-in-Publication Data
Richardson, Judith Benet.
Come to my party / by Judith Benet Richardson ; illustrated by
Salley Mavor. — 1st ed.   p.   cm.
Summary: Despite their fear of her roar and sharp teeth, jungle animals
Savi and Harold go to Rana the leopard's birthday party.
ISBN 0-02-776147-9   [1. Jungle animals—Fiction. 2. Leopards—Fiction.
3. Birthdays—Fiction. 4. Parties—Fiction.] I. Mavor, Salley, ill.
II. Title. PZ7.R3949Co 1993   [E]—dc20   91-16320

to Phil
and Rob

It was nap time in the jungle.
Savi slept standing up.

Harold's head was under his wing.
The wind sang a quiet song in the
trees and vines and flowers.

Suddenly, a loud ROAR shivered the air.
"What was *that*?" asked Harold.
He fluttered his wings.

A leopard crept from between the
trees. ROAR!
Savi trumpeted. Harold squawked.

The leopard disappeared into
the bushes.
"I'm afraid," said Harold.

"It's only Rana," said Savi. "She woke us up! Now we can play. Can you stand on one foot?"

Savi stood on one foot. Harold stood on one foot too, but he stayed up in his tree.

"What does ROAR mean?" he asked.

"That's how leopards talk," said
Savi. "Let's jump!"

Harold jumped high over the trees.
"The leopards are having a party
at the water hole," he said.

"Maybe ROAR means come to my party," said Savi. "Let's go see."

"Maybe ROAR means I'll eat you up," said Harold.

They peeked through the trees.
They could see the cake.

"I want to go to the party, but
we don't have a present," said Savi.

"What do leopards like?"
whispered Harold.
   "I can pick some flowers,"
said Savi.
   "I can weave them into a crown,"
said Harold, "the way I weave
my nest in the springtime."

He flew down out of his tree.

They wove a crown of trumpet
flowers and spotted leaves.

They carried it carefully down
to the water hole.

"Cake!" said Savi.
"Look at their teeth!" said Harold.

"Maybe you'd like to sit on my trunk," Savi told him.

The cake said *Happy Birthday Rana* in pink writing.
"I am glad you came to my party,"

growled Rana. She put on her crown.
"Happy birthday to you," sang Harold.
Savi trumpeted and the leopards roared.

Rana blew out her candles.
Then they all ate the cake.

Harold was the last to leave.
He ate every crumb.

DATE			